THE LITTLEST CANDLESTICKS

by Sylvia Rouss
Illustrated by Holly Hannon

PITSPOPANY

NEW YORK ◇ JERUSALEM

The Littlest Candlesticks
Published by Pitspopany Press
Text Copyright © 2002 by Sylvia Rouss
Illustrations Copyright © 2002 by Holly Hannon

Cover Design: Benjie Herskowitz

Hard Cover ISBN: 1-930143-48-6
Soft Cover ISBN: 1-930143-49-4

Pitspopany Press titles may be purchased for fund raising programs
by schools and organizations by contacting:

Marketing Director, Pitspopany Press
40 East 78th Street, Suite 16D
New York, New York 10021
Tel: (800) 232-2931
Fax: (212) 472-6253
Email: pitspop@netvision.net.il
Website: www.pitspopany com

Printed in Israel

To My Colleagues In Early Childhood Education

In recognition of their dedication and caring
for the youngest members of our Jewish community

Sylvia Rouss

For my father and mother in-law,
Clarence and Genevieve Hamilton

Holly Hannon

ALSO BY SYLVIA ROUSS & HOLLY HANNON

The Littlest Frog

The Littlest Pair
2002 Storytelling
World Award Winner

On The Seventh Day …

God completed everything that was created in the heavens and the earth. This was a very special day, the Seventh Day, the SHABBAT.

And God blessed the SHABBAT, and it became a day of rest for all the world to enjoy.

From: THE JEWISH CHILDREN'S BIBLE
Adapted by Sheryl Prenzlau (Pitspopany Press)

Each Shabbat, little Abby gazed at the sight,
Of the Shabbat candles and the beauty of their light.

Her mother's candlesticks were made of gleaming gold.
They had been her grandmother's, and were very old.

Her sister Dina's were made of earth-toned clay.
They had seven colored jewels, one for every day.

Her sister Rachel's were made of crafted metals.
They had swirly vines and flowers with fine petals.

Abby sighed, "I love Shabbat. I really do!
But Mommy, when can I have candlesticks like you?"

"Abby, just wait 'til you're a little older.
You'll have candlesticks," her mother gently told her.

The next week, Abby's teacher showed her preschool class,
Two little candlesticks made of see-through glass.

"These candlesticks, you must carefully handle.
Paint them first, and then put in a candle."

Abby took a brush and paint, but what was she to do?
She noticed her friend, Gila, was painting her glass blue.

She watched Sarah take her brush and paint a thin gold line.
Abby held her glass and thought, "Should I do that to mine?"

"Mommy's golden candlesticks are shiny as can be.
Maybe I'll paint a golden sun for everyone to see."

Next she thought of Dina's candlesticks, with jewels all in a row.
"Red and blue and green and purple – I'll paint a bright rainbow!"

She thought of Rachel's candlesticks, with flowers made of metals.
So Abby painted yellow daisies with delicate little petals.

Finally, Abby said, "There's still something I must do.
I will paint one last thing and then I will be through!"

When Abby came home from school, later that same day,
She dashed into her room and hid her candlesticks away.

Abby could hardly wait to see her family's eyes.
She would wait until Shabbat to show them her surprise.

On Friday, Abby's family prepared to bring in Shabbat.
Abby's mother made chicken soup in her covered pot.

Her sister Dina began dusting every room,
While her sister Rachel was sweeping with a broom.

Abby covered the table with a cloth of lace.
Then she picked some flowers and put them in a vase.

Dina came into the room and tweaked Abby's nose.
"Now it's time for us to dress in our Shabbat clothes."

Dina helped Abby dress, while Rachel combed her hair.
Then Abby waited for her dad in his rocking chair.

Mommy said, "Daddy will be home very, very soon."
Abby nodded happily and hummed a little tune.

Suddenly, she saw her dad standing by the door.
He'd brought home two challahs from the grocery store.

He smiled at her and said, "Hello, Abby dear.
Please go and get your sisters, Shabbat is almost here."

Abby called her sisters with excitement in her eyes.
Then she ran into her room to bring out her surprise.

She came into the dining room, happy as could be.
She held up her candlesticks for everyone to see.

"Look, I painted the sun, daisies, and a rainbow too!
But when I finished painting them, I knew I wasn't through."

"So I painted this small heart because I want to say,
Just how much I love Shabbat. It's my favorite day!"

Abby placed the little candles in her little candlesticks.
She sang the blessing as her mother helped her light the wicks.

Abby's sisters and father watched with sheer delight.
They couldn't help but wonder as they observed the sight...

*Was it Abby or her candlesticks
that lit up that Shabbat night?*

BLESSING FOR CANDLES

בָּרוּךְ אַתָּה יְיָ אֱלֹהֵינוּ מֶלֶךְ הָעוֹלָם אֲשֶׁר
קִדְּשָׁנוּ בְּמִצְוֹתָיו וְצִוָּנוּ לְהַדְלִיק נֵר שֶׁל

Baruch atah Adonoy Elohaynu melech ha'olam, asher kid'shanu B'mitzvotav, v'tzivanu l'hadlick ner shel Shabbat.

Blessed are You our God, King of the World, for making us holy by giving us Your Commandments, and commanding us to light the Shabbat candles.